# GRANDFATHER'S GARDEN

# GRANDFATHER'S GARDEN

## Some Bedtime Stories
## for Little and Big Folk

# David Loye

*Illustrations by A. Christopher Simon*

*Osanto Books*

Published in 2019 by Osanto Books
Carmel, California
www.davidloye.com

Cover art and illustrations by A. Christopher Simon

Softbound ISBN: 978-0-578-43090-4

Hardbound ISBN: 978-0-578-50902-0

eBook ISBN: 978-0-578-50901-3

Book designed and produced by
David Gordon and Lucky Valley Press
Jacksonville, Oregon
**www.luckyvalleypress.com**

Printed in the United States of America on acid-free paper that meets the Sustainable Forestry Initiative® Chain-of-Custody Standards.
www.sfiprogram.org

Dedicated
to all the kids, teens,
moms and dads
who wake up this world
to its everlasting wonder

# CONTENTS

## A Note to the Reader

Kids, teens, and moms and dads reading to kids, will occasionally find a quaint old word or odd reference to old movies they've never heard of in these stories. No problem. These are the spice to waken the curiosity that expands our minds. Google also has quick answers if you want them.

Thus spake the Mifwump.

# PROLOGUE

## GRANDFATHER'S GARDEN

I was a lonely child. I lived on a shelf in the closet at the bottom of the stairs. There it was that out of little scraps of sponge rubber I built my little village. There, squenched up on that shelf, curled around them like a mother bird hovering over her nestlings, I built my village out of red, black, brown, and white bits for my little people, green for little bushes and trees, and purple and other colors for my little houses and other buildings. There out of me and my tiny friends I saw endless stories of high adventure, heroism, and romance unfold.

Oh, I went to school, and doctors, and sometimes I played quaint old games like kick the can, spin the bottle, or tree tag with other boys and girls, but it wasn't the same. I was safe and snug there on the shelf with my little people and the wonder of the great doings that out of nowhere came to life in our own little world. It was like I was alive on the shelf but as empty as a ghost in that other world.

Out of the all too often horrifying hullabaloo of that other world, twice a week our little bubble was punctured by the roar of the quaint old vacuum sweeper right out-side the closet door.

First came the bang, then the snarl like the growl of a snuffling beast, then our little world's vast sigh of relief as the creature became only a tiny whine that poof like a candle went out.

And twice a day came the shower of dust shook loose by the pound of feet up and down the stairs.

And sometimes the door opened, and along with the whop of mind- blinding light came the whomp of shoes tossed into a clump on the closet floor.

So that was it for most of the year—and then it happened!

For every year at Christmas, as the gift I wanted most, I got to go stay and work with Grandfather in his Garden.

Eggplants big as elephants. Tap dancing stalks of cel-ery. A pomegranate that made of itself a big bass drum and walked around with a cheery boom boom boom fol-lowed by a string of tootling trumpet vines. And grapes as big as basket balls. Huge potatoes we scooped into boats we paddled around the lake with sliced carrots for oars. Even popcorn that on hot days popped itself and blue berries that picked and cooked themselves for the best of pies and pancakes. And best of all were the boys and girls that Grandfather invited, from all over the world, to show us how to grow the Magic Mush Melon that could feed billions of poor people for only a nickel a day.

Grandfather was a funny little man with crinkly eyes, a red nose, and a bouncing bush of frizzy white hair that stood out in all directions.

He could tap dance, and play the banjo, and, like normally never happened with grown ups, he could listen to your problems. And every night we all gathered around the campfire, and the moon came out, and the wind died down, and we sat there keyed up, quiet, giggling, waiting while the sounds of the night wove their spell.

Bats squeaked, whip-poor-wills moaned, owls hooted, and up from the lake came the lonesome long wild and crazy laugh of the loon.

Here are some of the stories he told as we bunched together around the crackle and whistling of the fire on those enchanted nights.

# THE CARNIVAL OF VEGETABLES

Once upon a time, there were some very, very, very poor children who lived in South America in the town of Boca Nieve de la Santo Teavaldo. Nothing good ever happened in their lives. They had to work in the fields every day. They couldn't go to school. They didn't have any shoes. It was just a very miserable life.

In one of the garden patches where they worked there was a string bean who became very concerned about them. His name was Georgio. There was also an older string bean whom they called Gramma Mama Mia, and one day Georgio said to Gramma Mama Mia, "I just wish there was something I could do for the poor children of Boca Nieve de la Santo Teavaldo."

Gramma Mama Mia said, "There is goodness in you, Georgio. There is a luminosity about your string beanedness that I have noticed from first when you were just a blossom on the vine. Think upon it. Nurture your goodness, and you will find a way to bring happiness into their lives."

Christmas was coming and the little children just looked so dismal because they knew Christmas was coming and they knew nothing was going to happen special this year. And little Georgio, the string bean, just felt awful about it. He said to Gramma Mama Mia, "What can I do? I just must do something for them this Christmas!"

She said, "There is goodness in you, Georgio. Think upon it, and a miracle will come to pass."

### The Christmas Miracle

And so it happened. As Christmas approached, all Georgio thought about was his wish to make them happy. And lo and behold on Christmas eve he felt a tingling inside him, and he felt a strange urge to take out one of his beans and touch it to the nearest vegetable.

The nearest vegetable was an eggplant. So Georgio touched his bean to the eggplant and it turned into an elephant! He said, "Gramma Mama Mia, look at what has happened! This eggplant has turned into an elephant!

And she said, "Georgio! Georgio! This is so exciting. You have magic power. There is magic in your beans." She said, "You can transform all the vegetables into a carnival. You can have a carnival of vegetables. And you can entertain the children."

So Georgio danced about the garden patch, and he touched one of his beans to a carrot and it became a ringmaster!

And he touched one of his beans to a potato and it became a great fine white horse!

And he touched one of his beans to a stalk of celery and it became a beautiful ballerina who could twirl on the back of the horse!

He touched another bean to some zucchini and they all became high wire artists and tight rope walkers. They would swing from swings and jump from place to place.

He touched a patch of parsley that had never amounted to anything, and felt very inferior to all the other vegetables— and his magic beans were by now so powerful, and he was doing so much good in the world, like Gramma Mama Mia said, that they all turned into lions and tigers. They roared, and everybody noticed them, and they provided a lot of entertainment.

He went into an onion patch and touched them with another bean and they all turned into clowns who would roll around and tell jokes, and go and sit in people's laps and make them cry — because even though they were clowns they were still onions, and this made people's tears run down their face even though they were laughing and happy.

All the poor children were just overwhelmed by this wonderful carnival of animals for Christmas eve. They were just wonderfully entertained for Christmas eve with all the wonderful animals performing for them.

## *Georgio's Children*

At the stroke of midnight all the animals, and clowns, and tightrope walkers, and the lovely ballerina turned back into vegetables. But the children were so happy they felt no regrets because at last something exciting and wonderful had happened in their drab little lives.

But unfortunately little Georgio in giving them so much pleasure had used up all his own energy. He had given all the beans out of his own self except one. And he was sinking. He lay there and could barely move.

Gramma Mama Mia came and wept over him. She said, "Oh Georgio, you're so good, and you've given your life to the poor children."

And he said, "Gramma Mama Mia, I don't mind to have given my life to bring a little happiness into this world."

Just at that moment, as he was sinking, and as Gramma Mama Mia was wringing her hands in despair, one of the little children who was leaving saw him. She said to another child who was her friend, "Oh look, there's a little string bean with just one bean left in it. Let's plant it in our own little garden and see what happens."

And so at the very last moment, Georgio was saved! The children planted his last bean in their own little garden. And of course a new string bean vine grew in that spot. And every year at Christmas one of Georgio's own children— the string beans who grew up from his own last bean— would once again go through the garden patch and touch the magic beans to all the vegetables.

And for that one night of the year, year after year after year, every Christmas eve there was this wonderful carnival of vegetables to delight the poor children of Boca Nieve de la Santo Teavaldo.

*A Moral for the Story:*
*"The desire to do good in the world*
*can work miracles."*

# THE CLAM THAT MADE
# A PEARL

This is the story of the Clam of Am. It comes from an old Indian legend from the Onega tribe and it was told originally 500 years ago by a chieftainess of the Onega tribe to her grand-children. This is the story of Ham the Clam.

Ham was a happy clam and just going about his business at the bottom of the ocean. Everything was going along just fine until he fell in love. The way it happened was that he was in his clam-bed and there were all these girl clams around him, but they just didn't interest him. He just thought, "You know, there's something about clams that's un-interesting. They're sort of mud-brown and lying around here in the mud, and, I just don't go for that." Then one day he saw this gorgeous sea urchin and he fell in love just BANGO! Like that. Instantly.

So he worked up his nerve and the next time she went by he said, "Pardon me, what's your name?"

And she says, "Me name is Shellaylie. Shellaylie Sea Urchin."

He thought that was the most lovely name he had ever heard and he said, "That is the most lovely name I've ever heard."

She felt very complimented and, well, to make a long story short, they fell in love, just BANGO, just instantly. And they saw no reason to futz around and within about five minutes they decided they'd go to her parents and he'd ask for her hand in marriage.

So, they went to her parents and the parents were, well, how should I say it — they didn't want to appear prejudiced, so when Shellaylie said to them this is my new intended, Ham the Clam, Mrs. Sea Urchin said, "Pleased to meet you." But within herself, she thought, "A clam? A clam for a son-in-law? No way, Jose!"

## Mrs. Sea Urchin's Plot

She knew that her daughter, Shellaylie, had an enormously strong will, and that unless she could come up with something that would stop this marriage, Shellaylie would prevail in the long run, particularly because her father was such a disappointment. He had the strange name of Mordred, which didn't fit him at all, as he was a rather harmless-looking sea urchin. He was a very quiet man who never said anything but "Yup!" or "Nope!"

So, she said, "My dear, your father and I really must give this a little thought overnight."

And Shellaylie said, "Well, all right, Mom, but I want your answer tomorrow."

That really put the pressure on. So that night Mrs. Sea Urchin said to Mordred, "We've got to do something!"

She talked at great length and she said, "Are you listening to me?"

And he said, "Yup!"

And she said, "You're sure you're listening to me?"

He said, "Yup!"

She said, "You're sure you're not thinking about something else?"

And he said, "Nope!"

So she said, "What did I say?"

And he said, "Well, my dear, you outlined a truly fiendish scheme. As I recall, you said you are going to invite your sister, Gertrude, over tomorrow, and get Gertrude to put an obstacle, an insurmountable obstacle, before this marriage."

She said, "That's very good, Mordred."

And that is exactly what she did.

### Aunt Gertrude to the Rescue

So the next day when Ham the Clam came back to get the answer to whether he could have the hand of Shellaylie Sea Urchin in marriage there was Aunt Gertrude all primed. And she asked Ham the Clam, "Do you have anything special you can do? Because it really will take a special person to marry my niece."

Ham the Clam said, "There's nothing special about me except for my love for Shellaylie."

Shellaylie beamed at this.

Then Aunt Gertrude sprung her trap. She said, "As you know, Shellaylie, I have been to the big city, and there I saw in the window of a jewelry store an oyster shell. Actually the two shells of an oyster that had produced a gorgeous pearl. I feel that my niece must marry a bi-valve that can produce a pearl, a gorgeous pearl as gorgeous as the pearl in that jewelry store."

Of course, immediately Mrs. Sea Urchin said, "Oh, that is such a wonderful idea, Gertrude!"

She nudged Mordred and he said, "Yup!"

Well, it was three against one—Ham I'm leaving out of

the equation because this was going by too fast for him. Shellaylie knew something was up, but it was three against one. She was about to protest when Aunt Gertrude pulled the Ace from her sleeve. She said, "You look like a young man of resolve. I think if you put your mind to it, you could produce a pearl. And then I could bless your taking the hand of my niece in marriage."

So Ham said, "Well, I'll try."

### Ham's First Labor of Love

So he went off and he asked advice from a very old clam. He said, "Have you ever heard of us clams producing pearls like oysters do?"

The old clam said, "I heard of such a thing maybe thirty generations back. There is this legend of Sam the Clam who produced a pearl. But no one has done it since that I know of."

Ham said, "Well, how do oysters go about it?"

The old clam said, "Well, the legend says that they get a grain of sand inside their shell that starts to rub around in there and it turns into a pearl. It just sort of scratches the pearl stuff off of the inside of the shell, and it sticks to the grain of sand, and builds up this way, and becomes a pearl over time."

So, Ham went to work at it. He swallowed some sand and it made it awfully uncomfortable sleeping with this grain of sand scraping up against his spine, but anything for love. So he worked and he worked and he worked and he produced a pumpkin! It was a miracle! He was so overjoyed! He rushed back to Shellaylie Sea Urchin's house and he said, "Look! I've produced a pumpkin!"

This sort of threw them for a loop and they realized they needed a little time to think about it. Mrs. Sea Urchin chopped up the pumpkin and made it into pumpkin pie and they had all the neighbors in and everybody said it was the best pumpkin pie they had ever had. Ham became very popular, but they still didn't want a clam for a son-in-law.

### Ham's Second Labor of Love

So Aunt Gertrude was called back in to do the dirty work. She prepared her sweeetest smile, and called the young couple together, and she said, "I'm awfully sorry to tell you this. We're very impressed with the pumpkin, but, well, it's not a pearl."

She thought that would end it right there. But Ham said, "I'll try again!"

So he went back and got another grain of sand and had to put up with it scraping against his spine at night and it was awfully uncomfortable and it took so long. But this time he produced a basketball! "Oh!" he thought, "It's another miracle!"

So he went back to Shellaylie Sea Urchin's house and said, "Look! Look what I produced! A basketball!"

Well, this was astonishing but also very disconcerting to Mrs. Sea Urchin. She still didn't want a clam for a son-in-law, but this called for some time to think it over. They took the basket ball out in the driveway where they had a basketball hoop on a thing over the garage door. They tried it out and all the neighbor kids came over and tried it out and everybody agreed it was the best basketball they had ever seen.

To top it off, it had the signatures of all the Harlem Globe Trotters on this basketball. There was a big write-up in the papers. The television stations came. Ham was really a pretty big thing. He even got on the cover of Time magazine.

But still, you know, he was a clam! And they didn't want a clam for a son-in-law.

## *Ham's Third Labor of Love*

So once again Aunt Gertrude was elected to do the job. She called the young couple together and said, "Now we're very impressed. Very impressed with your latest accomplishment, Ham. Truly we are. But it's still not a pearl. It's just not good enough."

She thought that would end it. But Ham said, "I'll try again."

So he went back and he and Shellaylie so much wanted to get married. It was so awful for them to be kept apart. Ham had put all his energy into these tasks. So, he went back and ate another grain of sand and put up with it scraping against his back at night.

Months went by.

Lo and behold, he produced an electric light bulb. He rushed back to Shellaylie Sea Urchin's house and said, "Look at here! Look at what I've produced!" They were really thrown for a loss now. We will need a little time to think this through, they figured, so they plugged the thing in and had to admit it was wonderful to have light at night. Because it was real spooky down at the bottom of the ocean at night when it got so black and you couldn't see anything. It was so nice to have this light bulb.

All the neighbors flocked around and said, "Oh, this is such a wonderful thing." The neighbors all sat out on the lawn and said, "Look at all the strange sea creatures that you can see at night with this light bulb." They had no idea of the wonders of the universe they were living in. Because there were all these things that came out only at night. But now at last they could see because of Ham's light bulb. This time he not only made it to the cover of Time magazine, but it was on CNN worldwide. They took pictures of all the things you could see at night with Ham's light bulb.

But still they didn't want a clam for a son-in-law. Father Sea Urchin—Mordred by name, you will recall—would have accepted him, but the mother sat on him and shut him up. She said, "Do you understand why we can't have him?"

And the father said, "Yup!"

She said, "You're not going to go wishy-washy on us, are you?"

And he said, "Nope!"

And she said, "You'll stick with the family on this, won't you?"

He said, "Yup!"

She said, "There'll be none of this male-bonding stuff, will there?"

He said, "Nope!"

So she figured that was all set, and so again Aunt Gertrude was elected to do the job. So she called the young couple in and said, "We're very impressed. The press attention is nice. It's been nice to stop and see all the sea creatures and so on, but, we're very sorry, it's not a pearl."

### Ham Succeeds!

Once again she thought that would end it. But Ham said, "Well, I'll try again"

So he went and ate another grain of sand, put up with its scraping against his spine at night for months. And lo and behold, he produced a pearl!

It was the stuff of which myths and legends would be made. His story would go into clam history through all eternity. Sam the Clam. Now Ham the Clam. Workers of miracles!

He rushed back to Shellaylie Sea Urchin's house and said, "Look! Look! I've done it! It's a pearl!"

Mrs. Sea Urchin didn't know what to make of it because she had never seen a pearl. Aunt Gertrude was gone, so she said to Ham and Shellaylie, "Well, we're going to have to call Gertie to get her back here because she's the only one that's seen a pearl. It could be anything for all I know. We'll consider it then."

So the young couple were just on tenter-hooks, just pins-and-needles waiting for the arrival of Aunt Gertrude.

The next day Aunt Gertrude arrived. She took one look at that pearl that Ham had worked so many months to produce. After all these tasks.

She took a look at that pearl that was one of the most magnificent accomplishments of the clams of all the ages. Only one other clam in all known clam history had achieved this. And she said, "That's not a pearl!"

She said, "That's a squidgy, squdgy, ugly, gray, mis-shapen awful looking thing. It's about as much like a pearl as a lump of coal is like a crystal ball."

Ham just stood there, frozen to the pavement.. And Shellaylie was speechless for a minute. And then she said—well, I really can't tell you what she said, because it was pretty raw and raucous. She just let Aunt Gertrude have it.

She said, "I've had it with you people! That pearl is good enough for me." And she swooped up Ham and they went off in a cloud of dust. Mrs. Sea Urchin and Aunt Gertrude just stood there blinking dumbfounded.

Mr. Sea Urchin did his best. He tried to look dumb and noncommital about the whole thing but pretty unsuccessfully.

And what happened to the pearl?

Well, of course, they made it into a wedding ring, which Shellaylie wore and passed on to all their children through 500 generations. And there it stands to this day, in the Sam and Ham Museum of Clam Wonders, which is located somewhere off the mouth of the Mississippi river in the Gulf of Mexico.

At least, this is what the old Indian legend claims.

*A Moral for the Story:*
*"Follow your heart and don't give up."*

# THE MIFWUMP

Once upon a time there was a creature that lived in the forest and it was a baffling creature even to itself because there were those who looked upon it and said, "Ahh! What a pretty furry creature." But others would say, "Oh no, its skin is as smooth as silk."

And others would say, "what a fine green thing." But others would say, "what do you mean? It's purple." Still others would say, "I would swear by a stack of Bibles that there critter is yellow."

Also, they seemed to disagree about how big it was. Some said, "Oh what a pretty wee thing!" But others said, "What do you mean? I see a fearsome giant."

So it was very difficult for everybody in the forest— as well as for the creature itself—to really get a fix on it, as they say.

Of one thing they were sure.

They would say, "Pardon me, but what's your name?" And it would say, "Mifwump."

They would say, "Mithwump?"

And it would say, "No, no! Mifwump!"

They would say, "Flumpflump?"

And it would say, "No, no! Mifwump!"

They would say, "Would you mind spelling it?"

It would say, "I have never learned how to spell."

So there was great difficulty even with the creature's name—even though it knew its own name perfectly.

## *The Lovely Princess*

Well, in this forest, deep in the forest, there was a lovely princess. Every eligible creature in the forest wanted to marry the lovely princess.

It wasn't just a matter of becoming royalty, thereby. It was just that the princess was so lovely that if you were at all eligible to marry princesses, you just wanted to.

It was just the thing to do.

And everyone, of course, assumed that the one most obviously ineligible creature in the forest was the Thumpthump.

As they were thinking this, the creature—which had abnormally sensitive ears—said, "I heard that. It's not Thumpthump, it's Mifwump." So, one had to be careful.

Well, time went by and one suitor after another would go by and see the lovely princess and try to win her hand in marriage. And the first one played a mandolin and she said, "That's very lovely, but it would not do for regular fare every night. I just can't marry you. I'm sorry."

The second one played the kettle drum. She listened for awhile, and then she said, "Well, that's awfully nice. I just love that rumbly sound. And when you turn the little handles on it and make the sound go up or down, it just sends shivers up my spine. But you just would not do for every night playing on the kettle drum. I'm sorry, but you will not do."

Well, the third one played the bagpipes. He set up this horrible squealing and wailing and everybody in the forest put their fingers in their ears, including the lovely princess. As he was playing, when he saw her put her fingers in her ears, he just stopped, and then quietly backed out of the room. There were tears streaming down his face because he knew he was no good, and there was no point in embarrassing her and in forcing her to deny him.

Well, it looked like she would never marry anybody. Because everybody in the forest who was eligible came by and oh, they danced jigs, and one could walk on his hands, and the next one could walk on one hand—just sort of hop on one hand. Others played the musical saw and some of them played mumbly-peg. There was even one of them who could jump through a hoop that was on fire. But the next day, of course, another one showed up who could jump through three hoops of flaming fire while swallowing a sword.

They just did everything. There was a tight rope walker. There was even one who was quite a magician. He could make himself disappear and then appear again, right there before your eyes. And he even made the whole forest disappear and everybody in it. There was nobody left there but the princess and himself.

He said, "See how great I am, O princess. I have made the whole forest disappear! There is nobody here but you and me."

But then this voice says, "And the Mifwump!" That shattered the illusion!

### The Test of Tests for the Mifwump's Magic

So the lovely princess said, "Well, if you were really any good, you could make the Mifwump disappear. But obviously the Mifwump's magic is stronger."

So the disappointed magician brought all the forest back, and all the people in it, and the castle and all, and slunk off to Philadelphia, where he played that night to a Christmas party for the Elks Club and tried to conceal his sorrow.

Well, it was cut down, really, to the Mifwump or nobody. So she called him in and she said, "Look, I don't want to be unmarried, all by myself, and not mate with anyone for the rest of my life. And you are the only one left. But, it's hard to know you. It's hard to know whether you're big or small, or fat or skinny, or what! I just wouldn't know what to make of you. I just wouldn't know what to expect day by day. I don't even know how to pronounce your name."

And he said, "Mifwump, Mifwump. M-I-F-M-U...M-U..." And he just broke down and wept and said, "I can't even spell it myself."

She said, "What are we going to do?"

And he said, "Well, you see, I've been put under a spell. I used to be a frog. And a wicked witch turned me into the Mifwump. The only way I can regain my original shape is if I can learn to spell my name. I've been practicing, but as you just saw, I can't even....I can almost think it, but I can't bring it off entirely."

She said, "Yes, well the point of it is, I don't want to marry a frog."

And he said, "But see, if I can get into the frog shape—you've heard this story of all the handsome princes that were turned into frogs? If I could just turn into a frog, maybe we could find a magic spell that would turn me into a handsome prince."

## *The Search for the Magic Spell*

And she said, "That is fascinating reasoning. I'll tell you what I'll do. I'll work with you and we'll try to learn together how to spell your name."

So they set out together to do this, and the first difficulty was that before they could spell his name, she had to learn how to pronounce it.

It took her a whole year to learn how to pronounce Mifwump. "Mifwump." She had to practice it. "Mifwump, mifwump, mifwump," she would say, over and over again like that.

Then it took a whole year to teach him how to spell his name. He'd go, "M-I-F-W-I-M-F..." Then he'd go, "M-I-F-F-...M-M-M-F-F-F..."

Finally, one day—and it was a beautiful day, the sun was shining and the birds were singing so sweetly in the forest, and the apple trees were all bursting with their apples--one day he said, "M-I-F-W-U-M-P, whereupon immediately he turned into a frog!

Well, they were so excited! Now all they had to do was to find another wicked witch who could change the frog into the handsome prince and they would be able to live happily ever after!

But search as they might, everywhere you could think of, they could find no one, and so he remained a frog.

And as time went by, she learned to love him just the way he was. And they were happy ever after—the frog and the lovely princess.

And as the years went by, she realized that she wouldn't have liked for him to be changed into a handsome prince, because she had grown to love him for his sterling qualities as a frog.

And that's the end of the story. . .

### *But Maybe Not...*

You want a different ending? Well. . .

He'd been changed into this frog, you see, and so they wondered and wondered about it. What could be the spell that would change him into the handsome prince?

They had a book that told the story of Harvey Firestone, who invented the rubber tire, like we have on cars. And they discovered that Harvey Firestone had discovered the tire by trial and error. He had this substance that became rubber, we call it latex today, it's a milky, sticky kind of stuff that comes from rubber trees. But although he could cook away the water in it and make it into something like rubber, that would bounce like rubber if you made it into a ball, it wouldn't last. It would just sort of fester and fiddle away.

So Harvey Firestone decided that he would mix this stuff with flour, and he baked it, and he hammered it, and he soaked it in acid. He did hundreds of different things to it. And finally, by luck—this is a true story, the true story of how Harvey Firestone gave us rubber tires and everything else that's made today of rubber— finally, by luck he added sulphur to this latex. He added sulphur, and heated it to just the right temperature, and it turned into rubber! But it took him years and years and years.

It was an unfortunate choice of books, this book that told them about Harvey Firestone. Because it was very difficult for the frog to be mixed with cornflakes, and then baked in an oven.

And then they tried covering him with flour, and smeared him with jam and baked him in that oven. Of course they always kept the temperature low enough so he wouldn't really get baked like a cake, but still it got awfully hot in there.

And they did all those awful other things out of the book about Harvey Firestone. He particularly didn't like to have to drink three quarts of sulphur and be baked at a low temperature for hours. But nothing worked.

## *The Great Transformation*

He was getting very worn out. He said, "You know, if I learn..." He gasped and tried to catch his breath and took a drink of water. "If I could just transform myself from a Mugwump..."

She said, "No, no, not Mugwump! Mifwump, Mifwump!"

And he said, "Oh, yes, Mifwump. If I could transform myself from a Mifwump by learning how to spell Mifwump, you know, M-I-F" —and he stopped. He was so worn out by being baked with all that sulphur inside him he had forgotten how to spell his own name again!

She took his hand and rubbed it with love. "W-U-M-P," she said, finishing it for him. "Mifwump. Mifwump."

"Oh yes," he sighed. "I was thinking that maybe I can turn myself from a frog into a handsome prince by spelling Mifwump backwards."

She said, "It's certainly worth a try, my dear."

So they had just an awful time spelling Mifwump backwards.

They both worked at it, and they just couldn't get the letters straight until suddenly she had a brilliant idea.

They got in front of a mirror, and they wrote the word Mifwump on a sheet of paper, and they held it before the mirror. And then they read from the mirror.

And there it was, and there they read it together. The magic letters "P-M-U-W-F-I-M" that spelled Mifwump backwards—and he was instantly transformed into the handsomest prince that ever lived. And they fell into each others arms and lived happily ever after.

### *You're still not satisfied?*

Well, all right. After the Mifwump and the princess found each other, and settled down, out of the great enduring surge of love and happiness that grabbed them the deeper side to the Mifwump emerged.

He became more playful, quite a cut-up in fact, and they had a lot of fun together, but in addition to the power of being all-seeing and all-knowing, there now moved out of him into the world the even greater power of being all-caring.

He began to look for places where people were

hurting rather than helping other people. Unseen he would swoop in to befuddle and divert the hurters and buck up and shore up the helpers.

Often it was too much for him—there were so many hurters, and so many helpers boxed in by hurters. But steadily his sense of what was right and what was wrong expanded ...

Meanwhile ...

*A Moral for the Story:*
*"Good looks aren't everything."*
*Or:*
*"Being clever isn't everything."*
*Or:*
*"Sometimes it takes a lot of trying to do something,*
*or a lot of experiments,*
*before you hit on the right answer."*

# THE MYSTERY OF THE DODO IN THE TUM-TUM BUSHES

Once upon a time, there was an auk named Dodo. And one day this auk, who happened to live in Australia—but of course it didn't know that where it lived was called Australia, all it knew was that it was living in this wide, wide wilderness that got awfully hot some times and awfully cold at other times..

Well, it was walking through the Tum-Tum bushes, for the Tum-Tum bushes grew very plentifully in this area of Australia, when it chanced upon a stream in which there was a creature.

The auk paused and said, "What are you?"

The creature, which was swimming in the stream, but then crawled up on the land, said, "I am a platypus. What are you?"

The auk said, "I am an auk named Dodo."

The platypus said, "You can't be an auk. Auks are extinct."

The auk looked at the platypus and said, "Is that a duck-bill that you are wearing?"

And the platypus said, "Yes, it's the latest fashion. It was given to me by evolution."

And the auk said, "If you are truly a duck-billed platypus, you are extinct."

This gave them both considerable reason for thought. The platypus looked down into the stream and saw its reflection and thought to itself, "I can't be extinct, because I can see myself there in the water."

### *The Mystery Deepens*

The auk sort of shook itself, and preened its feathers with its bill, and thought to itself, "I'm very much here and alive. I can't be extinct."

To make sure it did a little tap dance that raised up the

dust a bit, while it flapped its stubby wings. Sure enough, there in the dust were these footprints made by tap-dancing auk feet.

"If I'm extinct, how did I make those tap dancing footprints?" it asked the platypus.

"And if I'm extinct, why can I see my reflection there in the stream—and yours, too?" said the platypus.

They both granted that it was too much of a mystery to try to solve on such a hot day before lunch time and then nap time. So the auk continued on his way through the Tum-Tum bushes and all of a sudden he came upon a great saber-toothed tiger. Now fortunately the saber-toothed tiger had already eaten, but the auk didn't know this. The saber-toothed tiger looked at the auk and said, "What are you?"

The auk began to tremble and sweat ran down its face. "I'm only a harmless auk named Dodo," it said.

And the saber-toothed tiger said, "Aww, get off it, you needn't be afraid, I've just had my dinner. I'm not going to eat you." He said, "What'd you say your name was, again?"

And the auk said, "I'm just an auk named Dodo."

"Auk!" said the saber-toothed tiger. "Auks is extinct."

Before he had time to think through what he was saying, Dodo the auk made the mistake of saying, "Well, it was my understanding that saber-toothed tigers are extinct."

And then he made it even worse by saying, "And, by the way, it's incorrect to say 'Auks is extinct.' You should have said, 'Auks are extinct.'"

And then he realized he'd said the wrong thing, for the tiger's brow furrowed.

And then it wiped its face with one big paw.

And the auk stood there paralyzed, realizing that he'd angered the tiger, and that probably the tiger was considering whether it might not be nice to have a little dessert of auk al la mode.

## Saved by the Bee

At that moment, a bee came buzzing by and started buzzing around the saber-toothed tiger's head distracting it. It kept crinkling it's nose and waving at the bee with a paw that broke it's line of thought and it forgot all about considering the auk for dessert.

The auk felt that this was a good moment to sort of slip away. And so he did.

And so he walked and he walked. The truth be that he waddled, it wasn't much of a walk. It was truly a waddle. He was a really gawky, ungainly bird with every reason to be extinct. And so he waddled and he waddled through the Tum-Tum bushes and he came to the strangest creature and he asked this creature—who was an awfully shy round sort of bird with a sort of silly curve bill and nervous stupid look on its face. He asked what it was, and the creature looked awfully embarrassed and sort of crinkled its face and the auk could see it was thinking.

Finally the other bird said, "I'll think of it in a minute, now. Who and what are you?"

And the auk thought, "Oh, this must be the world's dumbest creature. It doesn't even know what it is." But the auk was very polite and so it said, "Well, I'm an auk."

The other one thought and thought and thought.

And crinkled up its face.

And scrunched its funny curved bill around.

And sniffed a few times, and scratched its foot in the sand, and then looked up at the sky and said, "Hmmmm, that's interesting." And then it looked puzzled and said, "I'm sorry, I just forgot, what did you say?"

The auk was a little put out.

"I'm an auk," it said. "An auk. A-U-K. Auk. Auk."

The other bird crinkled its face and said, "Hmmm, that's very interesting. And what did you say your name was?"

### Dodo and Dodo, Inc.

The auk said, and by now it was getting a little exasperated, this was not a conversation it was enjoying. It said, "I'm an auk named Dodo. Dodo. D-O-D-O. Dodo."

Now the auk could see that what it had said had lodged in some cavern within the other bird's diminished intellect, but still there was something going on upstairs.

One could almost hear the clanking of the gears, and the other thing sort of began to breathe a little heavily with the effort of thought.

Finally its eyes sort of bolted and it looked very startled and astonished and it said, "What did you say?"

And the auk said, "Dodo! Dodo! My name is Dodo."

And the other creature said, "That's me! I'm the dodo. I'm a dodo. I just remembered."

And the auk said, "That can't be, for dodos are extinct."

The other thing that thought it was the dodo had to think about this and it crinkled up its face and scrunched around and walked a bit and whistled a little. Then it sat down on a rock just looking so mournful. It said, "I knew there was something wrong with me. I just knew it."

It just sat there for the longest time.

The auk was about to go on but the dodo said, "Wait!"

It looked up, very sad, and wiped a tear from its eye. "It's probably true that I am extinct. I'm pretty dumb

I realize. But I'm not so dumb that I don't know that auks are extinct."

And the auk said, "You're the third person that's told me this. So It must be true." And he sat down on a rock next to the dodo.

Here were these poor two extinct birds in this area of the Tum-Tum bushes in Australia in which everything else seemed to be extinct: the duck-billed platypus, the saber-toothed tiger. In fact it was doubtful that the saber-toothed tiger had ever even lived in Australia. Maybe this wasn't even Australia. It was all very, very confusing.

And they sat there, the auk and the dodo, and gradually they found that being extinct together was a bonding experience.

The dodo put his wing around the shoulder of the auk. The auk wept a bit and put his wing around the shoulder of the dodo.

Then they rose, looked out beyond the Tum-Tum bushes into the vast wasteland. And they got up, their wings around each other's shoulders, and the dodo said to the auk, "Louie, this looks like the beginning of a beautiful friendship."

It was like something in a movie.

In fact it was in a movie. For that is what Humphrey Bogart said to Claude Raines in the movie Casablanca as they walked off into the desert together leaving the airport. But that is another story altogether.

### A Moral for the Story:
*"Nothing is really gone from us*
*as long as someone somewhere*
*still hangs onto it in their mind."*

# THE CARROT THAT WANTED TO BE A SPEED BOAT RACER

Once upon a time there was a baby carrot that wanted to be a speed boat racer. She realized that this might arouse scepticism among her peers, so she tried to sit on her feelings and not tell anybody. But this was not easy because they had this little game they would play among themselves.

They would say, "What do you want to be when you grow up?"

And one would say, "I want to be big carrot."

Another one would say, "I want to be a squash blossom."

Another one would say, "I want to be a grapevine." That was a strange answer. Why did this one baby carrot want to be a grapevine?

The little carrot's explanation was that it had grown up under a bunch of grapes, and the first thing it saw when it burst through the soil was this gorgeous thing like a chandelier hanging overhead of these reddish-greenish sort of round things on a stem.

It found out they were grapes, and it got to talking with one of the grapes, and quite a friendship struck up between them.

The baby carrot said to the grape, "You seem to have many brothers and sisters that you're interconnected with very closely by all those stems."

The grape said, "This is just the beginning of it. What you must realize is that I'm just one of a bunch of us. There's about 60 or 70 bunches of us on this one grapevine, and in this vineyard there must be maybe about 300 grapevines with about 60 or 70 bunches of us on each one of these grapevines. I am one of a family of million of grapes!"

This so impressed the baby carrot that she said she wanted to be a grape because she had to admit that, although she was in a patch of carrots, they weren't connected by anything. They breed sort of by themselves, in a sense, not interconnected intimately like the grapes were. The other carrots found that something to think about and talked about it for a good week.

Then they came to the little carrot who wanted to be a speed boat and said, "What do you want to be when you grow up?"

She decided to play it very carefully. She said, "Oh, I want to be a hat rack."

They said, "What's a hat rack?"

She said, "I don't know. It's just a word I heard that sounded interesting. A hat rack."

This game continued and one day when she was not thinking straight they came around to her again and said, "What do you want to be when you grow up?"

And before she could help herself she blurted it out.

"I don't care, just as long as I can be a speed boat racer."

### The Problem with Carrots

Well, this caused a great deal of laughter and derision in the carrot patch. One of them said, "Your chances of being a speed boat racer are absolutely nothing, zilch, in nowhere's-ville."

And the little carrot said, "Why?"

The other carrot said, "Well, for one, your name is Daisy. No little baby carrot with a name like Daisy could ever get a speed boat."

She said, "Why not? What's wrong with a name like Daisy?"

The other carrot said, "Well, if your name was Jane or Morgan or Radcliffe, you might have a chance. But a name like Daisy. It just doesn't go with speed boats."

She didn't like the idea, but she thought to herself, "Well, if that's what it takes, I'll change my name."

So she changed her name to Radcliffe. And a year went by and there was no speed boat. And so she changed her name to Morgan. And another year went by with no speed boat. And she changed her name to Jane. And another year passed, and still no speed boat. She had just about given up the idea that she'd ever get herself a speed boat when one day a very interesting thing happened. There was a rich little girl who had a wind up toy speed boat. And in a fit of rage this rich little girl threw the toy speed boat out of the window of her play room. And it fell into a stream that flowed for hundreds of miles. And finally this little toy speed boat got stuck in the mud right next to the carrot patch!

### The Toy Speed Boat

One night when they all got up from the soil and decided to dance in the moonlight—for that is what vegetables do when no one is watching on moonlit nights—they got up, all the baby carrots, and they were dancing around in the moonlight.

Little Daisy—for she had gone back to her original name by then—was whirling and whirling and whirling. And she got quite dizzy, and began to teeter around, and finally whirled right off into the water of the stream nearby. And as she was pulling herself out, lo and behold, she found herself right next to this toy speed boat!

It was a wind-up speed boat. There was this key on its side you wound up to make it speed through the water.

"My goodness! My dream has come true!" Daisy the carrot exclaimed.

She called out to all the other baby carrots, who came clustering down the bank around her to marvel at her discovery of the toy speed boat. But just then the moon sank out of sight, and the sun began to come up, and they all had to rush back up and plant themselves back in the ground before anybody caught them out there.

So the next night when the moon came out again they all popped out of the ground again and went down to the mud bank where the toy speed boat was stuck.

Everybody agreed that it was clearly Daisy's because her prayers had been answered. But there was this big problem because it was a wind-up speed boat with this big key coming out of it. The problem was how could they wind up that key?

It was a strong spring that would take human fingers to turn the key. Daisy could get in it and pretend she was racing, but there was no way to go anywhere because they just didn't have the strength by themselves to wind it up. And so once again it looked like Daisy would never realize her dream.

Well, one day a little farm boy was walking down along the shore whistling. And what he was whistling was the song that Jiminy Cricket sings in the movie of *Pinocchio* about when you wish upon a star. He began to sing it.

"When you wish upon a star, makes no difference who you are. Da da da da da da daaaaa daaaaa daaaaa."

He had a lovely voice and all the baby carrots cocked their ears to hear this lovely song. Then they were greatly concerned because they saw he had discovered the toy speed boat.

Somehow they knew he would pick it up and take it and poor little Daisy would never realize her dream!

And sure enough, as they watched, he picked it up and started to put it in his pocket. And then just as they thought it was hopeless, he stopped. He began to wind up the little wind up speed boat, for of course being a farm boy his fingers were strong enough to do this.

And do you know what happened next? The most amazing thing. For just as he finished winding up the toy speed boat there was an earthquake, and it shook him up so much he dropped the speedboat, and it fell onto the mud all wound up!

### *Daisy, Jiminy Cricket, and Greta Garbo*

Well, the little boy was so frightened by the earthquake that he ran off. And what the earthquake did was loosen up the soil so that all the little baby carrots were able to work their way up out of the soil even though it wasn't night time with the moonlight.

So they ran over, and all pushed together, and they got the toy speed boat in the water! And Daisy jumped aboard, and pushed the little switch, and went speeding up the river. Speeding up the river until she was out of sight.

For a long time they never saw her.

They used to sit around and wonder what happened to Daisy. And gradually it became a story that was handed down generation after generation among the baby carrots because of course it was the most exciting and mysterious of things that had happened among the carrots of that carrot patch. The story of this baby carrot who departed from their midst in a toy wind up speed boat.

Then one day it happened. A large Rolls Royce rolled up alongside the carrot patch, and out of it wearing an expensive artificial or faux mink coat and flashing huge diamonds stepped none other than Daisy Baby Carrot. They listened transfixed as she told her story of success.

It seems that when she was speeding up the river on her toy speed boat a Movietone news person saw her and filmed her speeding by. And this news film was shown in all the theaters— for this was back in the days before television, when the news reels were shown in theaters. It was shown in all the theaters and a big producer in Hollywood saw her and decided to star her in a movie, and she became as famous as Greta Garbo. But the nice thing about Daisy was that she never forgot her humble origins. She came back to the baby carrot patch and took all of them to Hollywood with her for a big tour.

And they all got to make their footprints in wet cement in the special sidewalk for the feet of movie stars, and to wear costumes and star in western movies as cowboys and Indians, and to sit on the top of the Hollywood sign on the mountain above the movie capital and sing the song that Jiminy Cricket sang in *Pinocchio*.

Out over the movie capital drifted the little carroty voices that made everybody feel good in the busy, glitzy city below.

"When you wish upon a star, makes no difference who you are, da da da da da da da da daaaaaaa daaaaaa daaaaaaaaa....".

### A Moral for the Story:
### "Don't let anybody laugh you out of something you really want to be or do."

# BABBAGE THE CABBAGE

Once a upon a time there was a cabbage named Babbage. And all that Babbage wanted out of life was to play Mumbly-Peg. His friends the Carrots would come by and they would say, "Babbage, let's go play soccer." And Babbage would mumble, "Just want to play Mumbly-Peg."

And his friends the Onions would come by and they would say, "Babbage, let's go play kick the can." And Babbage would mumble, "Just want to play Mumbly-Peg."

And his friends the Cauliflowers would come by and they would say, "Babbage, let's go swimming down at the old swimming hole." And Babbage would mumble, "Just want to play Mumbly-Peg."

One day a new creature appeared in the garden patch. She was gorgeous. All the vegetables were atwitter, wondering who she could be, and where she came from, and who, among all the single male vegetables, she might decide was Mr. Right.

The Corn said, "Well, of course, she will pick me because I'm the tallest and my leaves rustle with such majesty when the wind blows through the cornfield."

And the Pumpkin said, "Well, of course, she will pick me because I am the most beautifully round and orange thing and I have such a lovely long vine."

And the Watermelon said, "Well, of course, she will pick me because I also have a long vine, but I am beautifully green on the outside and an absolutely gorgeous red on the inside."

The Garlic said, "Well, I sort of think that maybe, well, maybe she might pick me." But they all laughed because they knew there was no chance for the Garlic.

So it went on in this way, with the Beets putting in their case, and the Potatoes putting in their case, and the Celery making a big thing about how it had the best crunch of all.

"There's nothin' in this here garden patch that crunches like a good stalk of celery," it said.

And the Eggplant, of course, who was extremely proud of himself because of his shiny purple skin, said, "Of course, she will select me."

### Bashful Babbage

But Babbage just sat there and said nothing because... Well, he did say something. He mumbled, "Just want to play Mumbly-Peg."

So what do you know, this gorgeous creature started through the garden patch and she paused before the Eggplant and then walked on. And she paused before the Pumpkin and thumped him, and then walked on. And she thumped the Watermelot and walked on. And when she came to the Corn, she got a big sneezing fit because of all the pollen from the corn tassels, so it was obvious she would never pick him because of a basic incompatibility there.

And so she went from vegetable to vegetable. She did pause for a bit before the Celery, and while he made his case that he was the crunchiest, she made a very powerful point that was talked about for days thereafter. She said, "What good would it be if we were to link up and your great attraction was your crunchiness? That would mean

I would have to bite you and that is not nice." And the Celery shook his head sadly and said, "I never thought it through properly."

So she finally came to Babbage the Cabbage and she said, "What's your name?"

And he says, "Babbage."

And she said, "Babbage the Cabbage. How quaint and delightful." She said, "And what do want from life?"

And he said, "Just want to play Mumbly-Peg."

She said, "What's Mumbly-Peg?"

This stopped him cold because he realized that he didn't know what Mumbly-Peg was. It was just something he had heard, and because he mumbled when he talked, he thought it sounded kind of good. "Mumbly-Peg."

## Cabbage and Cabbage, Inc.

She said, "You are certainly shy and not very forthcoming, but I detect in you something beautiful underneath your unprepossessing exterior."

Of course this made Babbage feel immensely good. He was very impressed with these big words "unprepossessing" and "exterior." With his mind expanding to grasp these big words, and under the glow of her attention, and the idea that anyone on earth could possibly find anything beautiful hidden within him, for the first time in his life he felt impelled to respond in some at least half way memorable way. And so there came out of him the kind of question that would just be routine for any other half way developed creature. But it represented an enormous step forward in social grace for Babbage the Cabbage.

He said, "What is your name?"

Reciprocity it was. Reciprocity was growing within Babbage the Cabbage. There was working up within him, out of being gloomily absorbed with himself, the recognition of another creature. He was moving into a self-transcendent growth stage. He was going beyond ego-boundedness. He said, "What's your name?"

And she said, "I am the Cabbage Patch Doll."

And so at that moment something clicked within both of them. Babbage the Cabbage, Cabbage Patch Doll. It was obvious that, although they looked so very, very different, there was a magical, mystical link between the two because of that single word: Cabbage.

## The Mumbly Peg Quest

And it was then that the Cabbage Patch Doll had a sudden inspiration. She said, "I don't know where this knowledge comes from, but I intuit that you have the potential to be a great mathematician."

And would you believe it, this proved to be true, for Babbage did indeed, because of her influence upon him— because she believed in him, because she ultimately loved him, because she evoked the best, the most unique, the most creative surge within him—he became the great mathematician Babbage, whose discoveries led over the years to the invention of the modern computer.

He also entertained the greatest scientist of them all, Charles Darwin, at one of his famous parties.

If you don't believe it, you can see it for yourself today in Wikipedia or any history book.

And they set out together arm in arm, humming a little tune and skipping with joy once in a while, to comb the world looking for the answer to the most persistent and questionable question of our time: what is Mumbly-Peg?

*A Moral for the Story :*
*"We all need somebody to see what nobody*
*else sees and believes in us."*
*Or:*
*"Wonderful things can happen to people*
*if you believe in them."*

# THUDGLINKA

Once upon a time there was a little flower that grew from a bulb in the ground in the spring. Of course, she wasn't a flower at first, she was just a little green stalk that came up from this bulb. She looked like a rather thick blade of grass at first.

And it was while she was at this early stage, not sure of what she was—whether she was a blade of grass, or whether she was an oat, or whether she was a tulip, or goodness knows what—that her parents named her.

Her father was named Thudglunker and her mother was named Thudglinka.

And the mother said to the father, "What should we name our little child?"

And the father said, "Why of course, my dear, we must name her Thudglinka because all our female children since the beginning of time have been given the name of the Thudglinka. If she were a boy she would be given my name, Thudglunker."

They both felt very good about this because they both thought that these were of course, naturally, the two most beautiful names on Earth.

And if the truth be known, they rather looked down their noses at all the other flowers around them that had other names like Mary, and Joseph, and Paul, and Mildred, and Hortense, and Hepzabah, names like that. As far as they were concerned, there was nothing prettier, nothing more harmonious, nothing more noble, nothing more gracious, or nothing more memorable than the name Thudglunker for a boy and Thudglinka for a girl.

And so it was that little Thudglinka Gladiolus was given her name.

## *Beauty and the Beastly Name*

She didn't think too much about it for a while as she was growing up, because she just steadily got a little bit thicker, and a little bit taller, and she was still green and could have been anything.

She could have been a jonquil, or she could have been a tulip. She was getting too big for a daffodil, but she might have been some kind of lily. But no one thought too much about it. They just accepted the fact that she was a Thudglinka.

But when she began to flower, she was just absolutely gorgeous. People began to notice her when the first flower appeared on her stalk. It was a glorious, luminous light shade of purple.

At first, people would come from all around and say, "My goodness. Look at that. Look at Thudglinka."

But by the time the next flower on her stalk appeared, also a glorious light shade of purple, someone said, "What an ugly name for such a lovely flower. Thudglinka., ugh, ugh, ugh!"

There were others who heard this, and it was whispered around, and it became the thing to say, "Isn't it just awful about Thudglinka? Such a lovely flower and such an awful, ugly name. Thudglinka, ugh, ugh, ugh!"

There was a particularly nasty little group of dandelions who would come by. They had made up a little song that went like this: "Thudglinka, Thudglinka, blanky,

blanky, blanky, blanky. Thudglinka, Thudglinka, aren't you an ugly one? Thudglinka, Thudglinka, blinky, blinky, blanky, blanky."

Of course this made poor little Thudglinka feel dreadful.

## The Glory of the Thudglunk Tradition

Her parents told her, "Just don't pay any attention to those people. Legends tell us they've been coming around us Gladiolas for centuries trying to put us down because we have the most lovely names in the world: Thudglinka and Thudglunker."

They told her legends of all the great Thudglunkers and all the great Thudglinkas. The Thudglunkers fought all kinds of big things, like dragons. And they climbed mountains. And they built railroads. And they were successful captains of industry. And at least ten of them had become President of the United States.

And the Thudglinkas had been among the most ravishing dancers of all time. They played harps in concerts. They were great actresses, famed for the ability for their voices to be heard even before the days of electronic amplification. Even if they uttered so much as a whisper they could be heard clear in the back of the great concert halls.

This would buck up little Thudglinka for a while. But then this dreadful band of dandelions, now joined by a bunch of ruffian thistles, would come by and hoot and holler and snicker and sniggle at her. And they would sing their little song: "Thudglinka, Thudglinka aren't you the ugly one. Thudglinka, Thudglinka, blinky, blinky, blanky, blanky."

## Thudtinkerbell to the Rescue

She was feeling very downcast about all this when one day her aunt came to visit. Her aunt's name was Thudtinkerbell. Thudtinkerbell was a lively soul and it made Thudglinka feel good just to see her aunt. She told her aunt of all the problems she faced because of her name.

"The legends of the Gladiolas that my dear parents tell me is some comfort," she said. "But my father tells of nothing but Thudglunkers who became President of the United States and things like that, while all the females of our species, the Thudglinkas, can become nothing but actresses or singers."

Her aunt, Thudtinkerbell, said, "My goodness child, it is lucky I came along because I have been working to correct that sort of distortion. Some of the Thudglinkas have been among the greatest mathematicians of their age. Others have been great novelists. Still others have founded mighty social agencies that have done much good in the world. And still others have been remarkable athletes and even heads of state."

Well, this made Thudglinka feel better for a time, but back came the dandelions and back came the thistles.

And now they were joined by a particularly noisy band of burr clover, absolutely the most vulgar and prickly of growing things. And they would march around her and sing their little song.

One day her mother noticed that her flowers — which had shot up one after another, climbing up her stalk until there were eight of these lovely blossoms — were beginning to droop.

"Oh, dear me. What can we do?" her mother said. "Poor little Thudglinka is beginning to droop with despair."

### *The Great Yearning*

The word was passed throughout the garden to all the Gladiolas. "Something must be done." And they focused all their yearning upon little Thudglinka. They yearned and yearned and yearned that something good would happen to buck up her spirits. But each day she seemed to be drooping just a little more.

And then one night when there was a full moon, down from the sky on a moonbeam came riding a little old lady no bigger than a thimble. She was riding an old fashioned tricycle on this moonbeam. She had yellow shoes and a polkadot dress and her hair was dyed green.

Normally someone would look ridiculous to be dressed up like that, but there was something charming and indeed a little touching and even more so quite fetching about this little old lady. As the moon crossed the sky, slowly the shadow from the house where Thudglinka lived passed on by and the moon was shining directly down on Thudglinka.

The little old lady on the moonbeam came riding down and sat on the leaf of a lemon tree close by Thudglinka and spoke to her and said, "Why are you drooping, my child?"

And Thudglinka said, "Oh, it's nothing."

And the funny little old lady with the green hair said, "No, it is something. I can tell. I've been watching. I've seen you drooping. Tell me what it is."

And Thudglinka said, "Oh, I really can't. If you're a magic person, there are so many other people in the world that need your magic. You should go and help them."

## Thudglinka's Reward

But the little old lady with the green hair said, "I am here. I am your very special, very own spirit critter and the magic I have is just for you. When you were born I was born and my sole mission in the universe is to wait in the moon until a time of great need emerges in your life, when all else has failed. And then I can come riding down to earth on a moonbeam and do one magic thing to make your life better. So the time has come for me to do this."

And Thudglinka said, "Well, if you must know, and if it is true that it is only I that you can help..."

And the little old lady said, "It is only me ...."

And Thudglinka corrected herself, "if it is only me that you can help, then I will tell you. It's my name, Thudglinka. I realize it's traditional, and I hate to be ungrateful to all the hundreds, maybe hundreds of thousands of Thudglinkas who have gone before me, and I don't mean to be disrespectful of a great tradition, but it is an ugly name. The thistles and the dandelions and the burr clover, though nasty, are right. It is an ugly name and an ugly tradition. And I am beautiful and I deserve better on this Earth."

And the little old lady with the green hair said, "You certainly do, my child. I am giving you a new name."

And she called out in a voice that was astonishing, such a big voice from such a little critter. She said, "Hear ye, one and all."

And everything in the garden woke up and sat up and rustled its leaves and got ready to listen. There was a twitter of wonderment, "What's going on?" And another twitter of "Hush, hush, hush." And they waited and then in this clear, compelling voice the little old lady with the green hair said, "I hereby take away the name of Thudglinka forever." And she wrote the name Thudglinka on a piece of paper and rolled in up in a little ball and rolled it between her hands and it disappeared.

And then she reached behind Thudglinka's ear and pulled out another little piece of paper that had something written on it. And she called forth to a grasshopper who came jumping over, and she gave the new piece of paper to him and said, "Here. Read this aloud. This is your new name."

## The Mumbling Grasshopper

And everybody waited with great anticipation. Nothing like this had ever happened in the garden before. And the grasshopper said, "mumble mumble." And everybody said, "What? What did he say?"

The little old lady said, "Speak up. Let's try it again." And the grasshopper said, "mumble, mumble, mumble, mumble." And the little old lady said, "We do appreciate the effort, but I'm afraid we must turn to someone with a stronger voice and much clearer diction." She called out, "Do we have a volunteer?" And a trumpet vine stood forth and everyone felt vastly relieved, for something like a trumpet vine would surely have a voice that would carry like a trumpet.

And so it was that there in the moonlight, while the whole garden waited and all was hushed, the trumpet vine took up the piece of paper and called out one word, "Gladys!"

It struck them so profoundly.

"Gladys Gladiolus!" the trumpet vine proclaimed. And everyone agreed it had the most glorious sound in all creation. "Gladys Gladiolus! Gladys Gladiolus!" they said.

And the word spread. They had her on television. She signed endorsements of all kinds of products. But they had to be good products.

She would endorse nothing that was substandard. You see, once upon a time there had been something called the Good Housekeeping Seal of Approval. But now people only bought or paid attention to things if they had the Gladys Gladiolus Seal of Approval. And sure enough, as time went by, and her image and the glory of her name became more imbedded and imbedded in the public mind, the day came when she was elected not only the first woman President of the United States. She had also become the first vegetable— or rather in this case, flower, and in any case the first plant life—Head of State in the world.

And the mumbling grasshopper, whose name was Arnold, became Secretary of State, and the Trumpet Vine became her chief confidante, head of the Party, and Premier.

That is the story of Gladys Gladiolus, once known as Thudglinka.

*A Moral for the Story:*
*"Girls can be President of the United States*
*or anything else they want to be."*

# FLIPPO THE DIPPO

The great difficulty in Flippo's life can be told rather quickly. It was a problem that she faced on the first memorable experience of her life. Flippo was rolling along the beach front and she bumped into a large sleepy seal and the seal went HOOONNNKKK!—in other words, a very big seal noise.

And Flippo said, "Oh, pardon me. I didn't mean to bump into you."

Of course the seal was enormous, a giant creature in comparison to poor little Flippo.

The seal finally opened its eyes, and looked a little bit startled, and it said, "My goodness, what are you?" And Flippo said, "I'm a dippo."

And the seal said, "Well, in all my born days, I never seen nothin' like this." And the seal turned to the next seal, whose name was Sadie, and the seal said, "You just got to look over here and see this thing."

And Sadie looked and said, "What is it?"

And the first seal, whose name was George, said, "It calls itself a dippo." And Sadie said, "Well, in all my born days I never seen nothin' like that."

Flippo thought to herself, "These seals are really not very stimulating company because they just copy each other. They are copycats. They copy what each other says." But she was very courteous, she didn't give any sign of what was going on in her mind. She said, "If you will excuse me, it has been stimulating talking to you, but I have a mission in life that I must get on with."

And before the seals could rev up their brains to ask a question—for their brains worked very slowly—Flippo rolled on.

A half hour passed and Sadie said, "George, I wonder what her mission was." And George said,

"HOOONNNK!" and went back to sleep.

Well, it was a beautiful day. There were people out on bicycles, little children running around with ice cream cones in their hands, and some had balloons. Every now and then a little dog would run around and yap a little. And Flippo rolled on and on, feeling purposeful, very purposeful, until she bumped into someone else.

This time it was an old gentleman.

### Reginald Morehouse Morgantheau

I suppose some people would have called him a tramp because his clothes were sort of baggy, torn and tramp-like. And he hadn't shaved, and he kept drinking on a bottle of wine and smacking his lips. But what nobody realized was that he was one of the wealthiest men in that town and this was just his way of entertaining himself.

Normally, he lived in this giant mansion. He had made an awful lot of money in sheep ranching in Australia. And he had a butler and three Rolls Royces, but he never felt comfortable with all that wealth. He had grown up in a very poor, run down area of Sydney, Australia. So his chief diversion, and really the most enjoyable moments of his life, were spent at the beachfront acting like a bum.

It wasn't wine he was drinking, it was actually grape juice. And he actually didn't have a stubble of unshaven beard. It was very odd, what he would do. You see he would sort of slather his face with library paste, and then he would take a little handful of sand and rub it over his face so that it looked like he had a beard. And the library paste would of course wash off easily when he went back to his mansion.

Well, he was sitting there and Flippo bumped up against him and he did a double take and he said, "What are you?"

And Flippo said, "I'm a dippo."

And the man, whose name was Reginald—Reginald More house Morgenthau was his full name. Some of his friends called him Reggie and others called him Margie. Well, Reginald looked at Flippo and said, "So, you're a dippo."

And Flippo said, "Yes, that is what I am."

And Reginald said, "How long have you been a dippo?"

And Flippo said, "As far back as I can remember."

And Reginald said, "Do you have brothers or sisters, or cousins or aunts or uncles, or anything of that sort? Or are you it? Are you unique?"

And Flippo said, "I'm it. I don't have brothers or sisters or cousins or uncles or aunts. I'm it."

And Reginald said, "Where did you come from?"

And Flippo said, "I just sort of materialized one day out of the seventh dimension."

### *Seven Dimensions!!!*

Reginald said, "There are seven dimensions?"

Flippo said, "Yes, on Thursdays."

And Reginald was absolutely fascinated. He had lived many long years. He had had a number of careers. He had actually been for a while a trail guide in the jungles in Brazil. In a still earlier period of his life, he was an accountant in a bass factory in Bombay. So you see he had gotten around. He was a sophisticated man, he knew the world and had seen many, many things. But he had never encountered anything like Flippo before.

And his entrepreneurial brain began to come alive again. He was seventy-five years old, and he had settled into being this rich man living this strange double life, beach bum part of the time, wealthy recluse the other part of the time. But Flippo inspired him and touched the entrepreneurial button.

He saw that he had the makings of one of the world's great attractions. The only thing of its kind on the Earth. And he said, "Tell me once again, what is your name?" And Flippo said, "Flippo."

And he said, "Tell me once again, what are you?"

And Flippo said, "I'm a dippo."

Reginald could see it in his mind: Flippo the Dippo — the Wonder of the Ages! Big banners! An enormous tent!

## *Flippo the Wonder of the Ages*

And so he said, "I have a wonderful idea! I will turn you into one of the major attractions of our time! You'll be bigger than Elvis Presley. I want you to come with me to my home. I will give you the west wing, you can live in the west wing. You will have your own servants, your own butler, your own Rolls Royce. All you have to do is sign this contract we'll draw up and you'll become the most famous being on earth."

But Flippo hesitated. You see, she was very tender-hearted and didn't want to disappoint this unusual person that she had bumped into.

"I appreciate your interest, sir," she said. "I truly do. And I can see that you are basically a good person, that you wouldn't be simply exploiting me for your own benefit because you already have all the money you want."

Reginald said, "That's very true. I see this as a public service to a world starved for something different and hopeful."

But Flippo said, "I'm very sorry, but I have to be going on. I have a special mission on this earth."

And poor Reginald—or rather this very rich man who just looked poor — sank back on his bench and felt hopeless and helpless.

And so Flippo rolled on. And it wasn't until she had rolled clear out of sight that Reginald slowly came to realize something. There was a little boy with an ice cream cone standing near by, and Reginald said, "Son, I didn't ask her what her mission is."

The little boy with the ice cream cone didn't know what to make of this so he walked away very rapidly.

## *Ralphy*

Meanwhile Flippo was rolling on along the beach front, enjoying the sights and all of a sudden she bumped into someone else who was sleeping in the park on the ground. He sat up and rubbed his eyes, and he was a very nice looking young man, but obviously a little down on his luck if he was sleeping on the ground in a park.

He looked at her and said, "My goodness, I've never seen anything like you. What are you?"

And Flippo said, "I'm a dippo."

"And you can talk?" the young man said.

And Flippo said, "Yes." She said, "I can also zip." And she zipped.

And the young man said, "My goodness, I've never seen anything like that." And Flippo said, "And I can dLO." And she dropped.

And the young man said, "My goodness, I've never seen anything like that." He said, "As a matter of fact, what you remind me of, only you are doing it without an airplane, is a loop to loop that you can do in an airplane. I know this because, I may not look like it now because I've been out of work for months, but I'm a pilot. I'm a stunt pilot actually, but the promoter who was promoting me is a crook and he took all our money and ran off and I am having an awful time finding another promoter. I can fly the plane and do the stunts, but I am too shy to do anything about promoting myself. In fact,

I don't understand how I am speaking so openly and freely to you. Usually talking to anybody is so painful for me I can hardly do it."

And Flippo said, "Yes, I know. That's part of the reason I'm here." And the young man said, "How do you mean?" And Flippo said, "That's part of my mission."

## *Flippo's Mission*

And the young man said, "What is your mission?"

And Flippo said, "To spread joy. I have come into the world to spread joy."

And the young man said, "How incredibly beautiful. I just wish there was some way I could go with you and help you."

And Flippo said, "I see it all. It's in a vision that has come to me. Come with me." And the young man, whose name was Ralphy, hesitated because he never had encountered anything like this person from the seventh dimension. And so they went back along the beach front to where Reginald was sitting.

There was poor old Reginald sniffling and moping and once in a while sobbing quietly to himself, his dreams, his great entrepreneurial urge stifled. He was looking at this bottle of grape juice and wishing that it was wine, and he was thinking that this was really silly to sit on the beachfront with his face slathered with library paste and sand for a beard.

His eyes brightened when he saw Flippo and the young man.

Flippo said, "I have returned because I have found 50 percent of what I need for my mission."

And the old man said, "Oh, what is your mission?"

And Flippo said, "To spread joy in the world."

And the old man said, "Oh, how beautiful. I wish there was some way I could help you do this and go with you."

And Flippo said, "There is. Take up your bottle and follow me."

So the old man and the young man followed Flippo along the beachfront and into a taxi cab and to an airport where, under Flippo's instructions, the old man who looked like a bum produced an enormous wallet just bulging with money. And the old man bought the airplane and they got inside and took off under Flippo's instructions to fly over New York City.

And as they flew, out from the plane, in giant sky writing put by put, came the great letters in gratitude proclaiming the celebration of the gift of life on earth.

## *Joy to the World*

The people looked up and said "Joy! It says joy in the sky!"

People in the Bronx looked up, and people in Stanton Island, and clear up into Connecticut they saw joy in the sky.

Flippo, and Ralphy, and Reginald left the United States and went in the plane to Europe, and they flew over all the cities in Europe sky writing JOY in the sky.

And people began to be better. They would speak respectfully to each other and they would say, "Did you see it in the sky?"

"Yes, yes, I saw it. Wasn't it wonderful!"

They flew over Africa and Flippo knew every language. Over every country and region she would translate and tell Ralphy how to spell out JOY in Swahili and in all the other languages of Africa. And they flew over India, and China, and Japan. They even flew over little tiny places out in the Pacific that nobody ever went to. And everywhere they spread joy.

It was the most wonderful thing, everybody agreed, the most wonderful thing that had happened to humanity in hundreds of years.

Reginald was happy, and Ralphy was happy, but the happiest of all was Flippo the Dippo, who had brought joy to the world.

### *A Moral for the Story:*
### *"Friends are important."*
### *Or:*
### *"No matter who you are, one of the most important things you can do for everybody is to spread joy."*

# TUMBLING TUMBLEWEEDS

Once upon a time there was a tumbleweed in the desert named Myrtle, and the first thing that Myrtle decided was that she didn't like her own name. So she said, "Henceforth I will be called Muriel."

The second thing she didn't like was that she just didn't like this business of flopping around on the desert every time the wind blew, for that is what happens with tumbleweeds. Every time the wind blew all these tumbleweeds would take off and flop around the desert, and then bang up all together and form a clump, and then they'd be blown apart again.

Muriel told a friend of hers, another tumbleweed named Baxter, what she thought about this arrangement.

"Baxter," she said, " if I ever get a chance I'm going to stop this business of being blown around the desert by every passing wind and not having roots in anything! This is no life!" she said.

And Baxter said, "You're right, Myrtle."

"Now wait, Baxter, " she said. "Remember what I told you."

"Yes, yes, I'm awfully sorry, Myrtle, I mean Muriel." he said. "I'm with you there, Muriel, but I don't know how we can ever do it. We're just tumbleweeds, and that's the way it's always been with tumbleweeds, always is, and always will be.

"Like in the song in old western movies with Roy Rogers and Trigger and the Sons of the Pioneers, we're 'tumbling tumbleweeds.' It's the tumbleweed thing."

But Muriel said, "I don't care if that's the way it's been ever since time began. I've had enough of the situation and I'm changing it first chance I get."

Well, the months passed by. Every wind storm blew them apart, and then they'd get clumped together again, and then blown apart again, and sometimes she wouldn't see Baxter for weeks. Then another wind would come, and there he would be, blowing around the corner of a house toward her.

She was always glad to see him. She kept thinking that her chance would come in January or February when the rains came. You see, she had formulated a plan. Her plan was that when the rains came she would try to sink her roots into the ground long enough so that her roots would get so strong they could hold her in place when the wind came. She wanted to tell Baxter her plan, but he'd been blown off somewhere.

One day the winds came up and she saw him coming around the house toward her. Oh, she was so happy because at last she could tell him her plan and maybe they could root together somewhere.

He came swooping up on the wind and bumped up against her and said, "Muriel, how wonderful it is to see you!"

And she said, "Baxter, all these weeks there has been something awfully important I've wanted to tell you."

And he said, "Yes, yes, there's been something awfully wonderful I want to tell you, Muriel." And he began a long story. It was all about how he'd been blown out on the water, and then swept ashore, and how he'd been blown down a highway between a thousand cars and trucks and almost run over a zillion times. And he went on and on and on, and every now and then she would say, "Well this is all very interesting, Baxter, but I just want to say..."

And he'd say, "Please, please, Muriel, don't interrupt."

He would say, "Muriel, what you've got to understand is that when I'm wound up this way, when I haven't seen you in such a long time, why you've just got to sit there and listen for a little while, at least. Let me have my say."

And so he was starting to launch onto a tale of how he was blown up on a truck bed of a big truck that was carrying cars to Wyoming when another big wind came up. And she was just saying, "Baxter, please, I've got something important to tell you..." But the wind blew him away.

### Stopped by the School Bell

She didn't see him again for weeks, and she said to herself, "When I see him again, before he can open his mouth and go off on another long story, I'm just going to say real fast, 'Baxter, when it rains, sink your roots, try to get near me, sink your roots, OK?'"

So all of a sudden she saw him come blowing around the edge of a school building, and she was so glad to see him, and she called out "Baxter!"

And he called out, "Muriel!"

She was just revving up to tell him when the school bell rang, and all these children came running out from the school for recess. They ran right between Baxter and Muriel and for a while she couldn't see him at all because of this mob of school children shooting past.

And when they had all passed, he was gone. He had been blown off again somewhere.

Well, it went on like this another time. She was blowing about and she saw Baxter. They were just across from each other, on either side of a railroad track.

She called out, "Baxter!" And he called out, "Muriel!" But just like it had happened with the school children, a train came rushing by. And by the time it had passed, she had been blown off one way and he had been blown off in another direction.

Well, the rains came and she hadn't had a chance to tell Baxter about her plan. She didn't see him anywhere. She thought to herself, "Well, even though I hate to root myself in the ground without Baxter, the most important thing for me to do is to establish something new and different for tumbleweeds. Roots. Deep roots in the ground."

So when the rains came and the ground got all squishy and soft, all the other tumbleweeds just flopped around as usual. But Muriel worked very hard and shoved her roots into the soil, and then she concentrated on making her roots grow as fast as possible. And sure enough, she was able to root herself so that when the first big wind came and all the other tumbleweeds blew off, Muriel remained rooted in the soil!

But as the months went by, she began to wonder if she had done the right thing after all. On one hand she was feeling good about the fact that she had succeeded in rooting herself in the ground, so she couldn't be blown away. But on the other hand she was feeling lonely because she was there all by herself.

## The Difficulties of Being the First To Do Something

Once in a while the wind would blow and a tumbleweed would come tumbling around, but they hardly recognized her any more. You see, instead of being all dried out and dusty and gray as was normal for tumbleweeds, with her roots firmly in the ground to get water regularly Muriel was now a bush with leaves and green and yellow.

She tried to talk to her old friends among the tumbleweeds, or just anybody who came blowing by, and they were polite, but she could see that they felt she'd changed so much that they didn't have anything in common with her any more.

So a year or two passed, and she was increasingly lonely. She thought often of Baxter and wondered if she would ever see him again. She realized then that making her choice to try to advance evolution— to try to advance tumbleweeds up the scale of life, to try to give them roots somewhere—she had probably cut herself off from all the rest of her species.

It was very sad for her, but she took what comfort she could in being a pioneer.

And so it was that there came up a tremendous storm and the ground shook. It wasn't just a storm, it was an earthquake. And the ground shook and roared and great cracks appeared and buildings fell down, and everything from soup to nuts went flying off in all directions. And it just rained and rained and rained and the wind blew.

And one morning she woke up and to her great surprise there was Baxter.

## Baxter's Return

He'd been blown for miles and his roots were sunk in the squishy ground right next to her! When he woke up he was so glad to see her. He said, "You've changed, Muriel. I just wonder what we have in common now. You're so fresh and lovely, all green and yellow, and I'm such a poor dried out and gray old thing."

"Don't fret, dear," Muriel said. "You look lovely beyond description to me. Please now work, work, work to keep your roots stuck in that mud, and to draw strength and sustenance from the ground, so you can stay there when the winds come."

And so he did, and he was beginning to turn just a little green when the winds came. He tried to hold on. He said, "Muriel, I'm trying."

She said, "Yes, yes, you must hold on, Baxter!"

And he said, "I'm trying, Muriel, but it's an awfully strong wind!"

And it looked like the wind was going to blow him away. His voice was getting weaker and weaker, and finally he said, "Muriel, I can't hang on any longer."

And she thought for sure that all was lost. But just at that moment a milk truck came by and it parked in such a way that it cut off the wind from blowing on Baxter! And Baxter was able to hang on! It was because of the way the milk truck was parked, blocking the wind. And he was able to hang on, and soon he began to turn green and yellow like her. And then after a bit they began to have their own little tumbleweed children, and so Muriel and Baxter's whole family began to spread out from them, all green and yellow.

They still thought of themselves as tumbleweeds, of course. Only now they weren't tumbleweeds anymore.

### Clement T. Middlecamp and
### Phoebe Q. Mollendorf and
### Murielantis and Baxteronis

A professor came by. He didn't realize what they had been before and he announced that he had found this new plant that was a lovely green and yellow and was distinguished by it's awfully strong roots wherever it was planted. And he wondered what to call it.

His name was Professor Middlecamp. Professor Clement T. Middlecamp. He taught at the University of Michigan in the winters. In the summers he taught at the University of Missouri. Dr. Clement T. Middlecamp wondered what to call this new species of plant that he had found, and one night in a dream there appeared to him a lonely tumbleweed, tumbling over the desert. And the strangest thing happened, for this tumbleweed had a voice. And this tumbleweed said in a far off, squeaky little voice, "Dr. Clement T. Middlecamp, I have a name, and that name shall be your name for the species of this new organism. I am Muriel the Tumbleweed, only now I'm no longer a tumbleweed. You shall call me Murielantis."

And so it was when he woke up, he wrote down the dream and said, "That's very strange. It's almost as if it were real. As if it had really happened." And he announced to the scientific world the discovery of this new plant that was to be called Murielantis.

And Dr. Clement T. Middlecamp met a wonderful woman and they became married and she had a dream. And in her dream another tumbleweed appeared and said, "My name is Baxter and I used to be a tumbleweed, but now I'm a new species called Murielantis, but that's only part of it. I too, Baxter, was involved in this process of evolution, and all these former tumbleweed children are partly mine. Remember, " he called to her out of the dream in a far off little voice, "My name is Baxter."

Professor Clement T. Middlecamp's wife's name was Professor Phoebe Q. Mollendorf, for they had both kept their original names. So Phoebe Q. Mollendorf told Clement T. Middlecamp of her dream and they decided to call the new species of tumbleweed Murielantis and Baxteronis.

So that became its name in the real world, and this was quite an honor, but there was a problem. For there still yearned within Muriel and Baxter for something they could still feel even though they didn't know what or why. For now their name was shrunk to little more than a wan Latin phrase as withered and dry on the page as Muriel and Baxter had been in their earlier life in storyland.

And so it was that in the miraculous way the real world is connected to storyland they left the page that honored their contribution to evolution to shoot out into the unknown to live forever, and plump and green and yellow and loving each other, they populated vast continents of desert into lush new lands in the mind.

*A Moral for the Story:*
*"Sometimes it takes a long time*
*to get outof life what we want."*
*Or:*
*"Something in the world is working in*
*favor of true love, no matter how hard this*
*may be to believe at times."*

# PHYLLIS THE TALKING PILLBOX

Once upon a time there was a pillbox named Phyllis. No one could remember when Phyllis started talking so much. Seemed like she had been talking for as far back as any of the toys lived, for Phyllis the pillbox had been retired from duty as a pillbox and was now one of numerous strange household objects that had drifted into the children's room and wound up being used by the children as building blocks and for other uses.

There was an old battered green sauce pan that they used sometimes as a house and other times as a boat. There was an old brown cookie tin that was a little warped that they used to make thunder and rain sounds.

Whenever you tried to bend it straight it would make these lovely sounds like thunder when they wanted to pretend it was raining.

There was an old egg beater with a crank on the side that they used in the bathtub, pretending it was the motor on their motor boat.

But back to Phyllis the Talking Pillbox. Sometimes they would pop open her lid and put pennies inside her. But Phillis would say, "Oh, they are too heavy. Please don't put pennies in my tummy." So they would take them out.

Sometimes they would pop open her lid and put feathers inside her. But Phylis would giggle and say, "Oh, these feathers tickle too much. Please don't put feathers in my tummy." So they would take them out.

Most of the time they just listened to Phyllis, or didn't listen to Phyllis, for she could go on talking for hours.

She talked a lot about Idaho. When they didn't listen it was pleasant just to have her chattering away there on the shelf, for this made the children feel they were never alone. One could also depend on Phyllis to be their friend.

Well, one day a little man came down the street with a monkey. He was an old fashioned organ grinder, like you hear about in stories but never see anymore. He was looking for Phyllis,. As he went down the street he would call up to the people in the houses, or to open windows where somebody might be inside to hear him.

"Hellooooo there. Hellooooo there," he would call up, and the children heard him. "Hellooooo there," he called up to everybody. "Has anybody up there seen my pillbox?"

So they wondered what to do. Was Phyllis the pillbox he was looking for?

Should they stick their heads out the window and tell him about Phyllis?

What if he was just trying to get stuff from people? It was quite a dilemma. They looked around the room. But neither the battered green sauce pan or the brown warped cookie tin were any help, for they couldn't talk.

So what they did was...what they did...you see the sun was coming up, and it was Thursday...

But the story teller had fallen asleep, and started to snore. And so, open ended, the story spun on and on to reach beyond the moon and the stars.

### *A Moral for the Story:*
*"If you want to finish anything,*
*don't fall asleep before it gets done."*

# EPILOGUE

## CALL THE MIFWUMP!

Jumping Jehosephat! Heaven's to Betsy! Holy cow! Or shut my mouth and call me another one of Grandfather's quaint old exclamations. For just as I thought I'd finished this book the door blew open and I discovered the Miffwump wasn't just a story in this book. It was real!

There it was, the all-seeing, all-knowing, all-powerful Mifwump, hopping mad and ready to lead a revolution.

"The way you people in the real world are loading up with awful problems," and his voice shook the walls and rattled the windows, "we just can't take it any more. It's time for the best of us in storyland to break out into your world to save you with Miffwump Power!"

And what is this? As I've learned to use Mifwump Power in my own case, I've found that whenever I'm down in the dumps, fearful, apprehensive, anxious, or even reduced to despair, I just pick up this book and go back and reread one or more of Grandfather's stories.

No matter how awful something seems, up comes a chortle, then another, and then the great laugh that takes me out of my troubles into the playful wonder of *Grandfather's Garden*.

"I think you're on to something," I told the Mifwump, "but how can you get what seems to work for me out there to other people who need Mifwump Power to help keep them going in the worst of times?"

Thereafter out of the Mifwump emerged the gripping story of adventures as astounding as any of those Grandfather told us on those enchanted nights by the fire.

The first tale, as I recall, was about how the Mifwump and Flippo the Dippo left storyland to launch a revolution of *Joy* versus *Gloom* in the real world. For the inside story, step by step, use **Mifwump** as the search word for Google, YouTube, Facebook, Twitter, and other portals for the internet!

Help bop **Gloom** and spread *Joy* to the world!

Kids, teens, moms and dads, join up and tell your friends. And their friends. And their friends' friends. Help the Mifwumpians make new friends to spread the laugh of joy versus gloom all the way around the world on back to wherever you are!

THE END

# NOTABLE KNOWABLES

## THE AUTHOR

A grandfather with four grandchildren, great grandfather of one now, more pending, David Loye is a psychologist and evolutionary systems scientist. Author of the National Award winning *The Healing of a Nation* and many other books, he is best known for his recovery of the long ignored rest of Darwin's theory of evolution—that is, the Darwin who wrote 95 times of love and 92 times of the moral sense, not survival of the fittest, as the prime driver of evolution. Still a work in progress, Loye's major work remains the development of a new Darwinian moral transformation theory. He lives with his partner Riane Eisler, author of the international best selling *The Chalice and the Blade*, in Carmel, California.

His website is www.davidloye.com.

## THE ILLUSTRATOR

Grandfather of "a very talented young lady and irresistible twins," Alan Christopher Simon has worked 60 years in book publishing as a designer and illustrator, including classics by Dickens, Joseph Conrad, John Steinbeck, Evelyn Waugh... The rare delight of his brush has enlivened a long string of books during his seven years on staff at Doubleday, two years as art director and production manager for Clarkson Potter, twenty freelancing for at least 22 publishers, and twenty years at Easton Press as designer and illustrator. He lives with his partner, the distinguished watercolorist Wendy Hall, in the village of Leucadia, near San Diego.

## OSANTO BOOKS

Osanto Books is a new imprint that in a world gone off track has been formed to gather in one place books of the rare blend of love, laughter, and rock firm moral sensitivity we need to get back on track in evolution.

## ACKNOWLEDGMENTS

For their invaluable encouragement over the years our heartfelt thanks to Riane Eisler, David Gordon, Raffi, Wendy Hall, Jenella Loye, Chris Loye, Kate Loye, Evan Derrickson-Loye, Jon Loye, Kathy Loye, Chris Loye II, Kenny Loye, Hudsynn Loye, Owen Michael Loye, Ali Sellers, Cameron Ritchie, Andrea Eisler, Brett Ritchie, Loren Alison, Lou Roberts, Kim Pizor, John Mason, Claire and Patrick Clelland and their daughter Cassidy Clelland, and Christine and Eric Simon and their children Colin and Grace Simon.

Further thanks to Ervin Laszlo, Ken Wilber, Robert J. Richards, Stanley Kripner, Ralph Abraham, Fred Abraham, Allen Combs, Darcia Narvaez, Hazel Henderson, Ruth Richards, Barbara Marx Hubbard, Jeff Saltzman, Thom Hartman, Ray Bradley, and the late Karl Pribram and Paul MacLean...

and the once lost but now again found grandfatherly enduring presence, thought and voice of Charles Darwin.

Published by Osanto Books
P.O. Box 223384
Carmel, CA 93923

Softbound, hardbound, and ebook editions
designed and produced by
David Gordon & Lucky Valley Press
Jacksonville, Oregon
www.luckyvalleypress.com

CPSIA information can be obtained
at www.ICGtesting.com
Printed in the USA
FSHW022254290619
59498FS